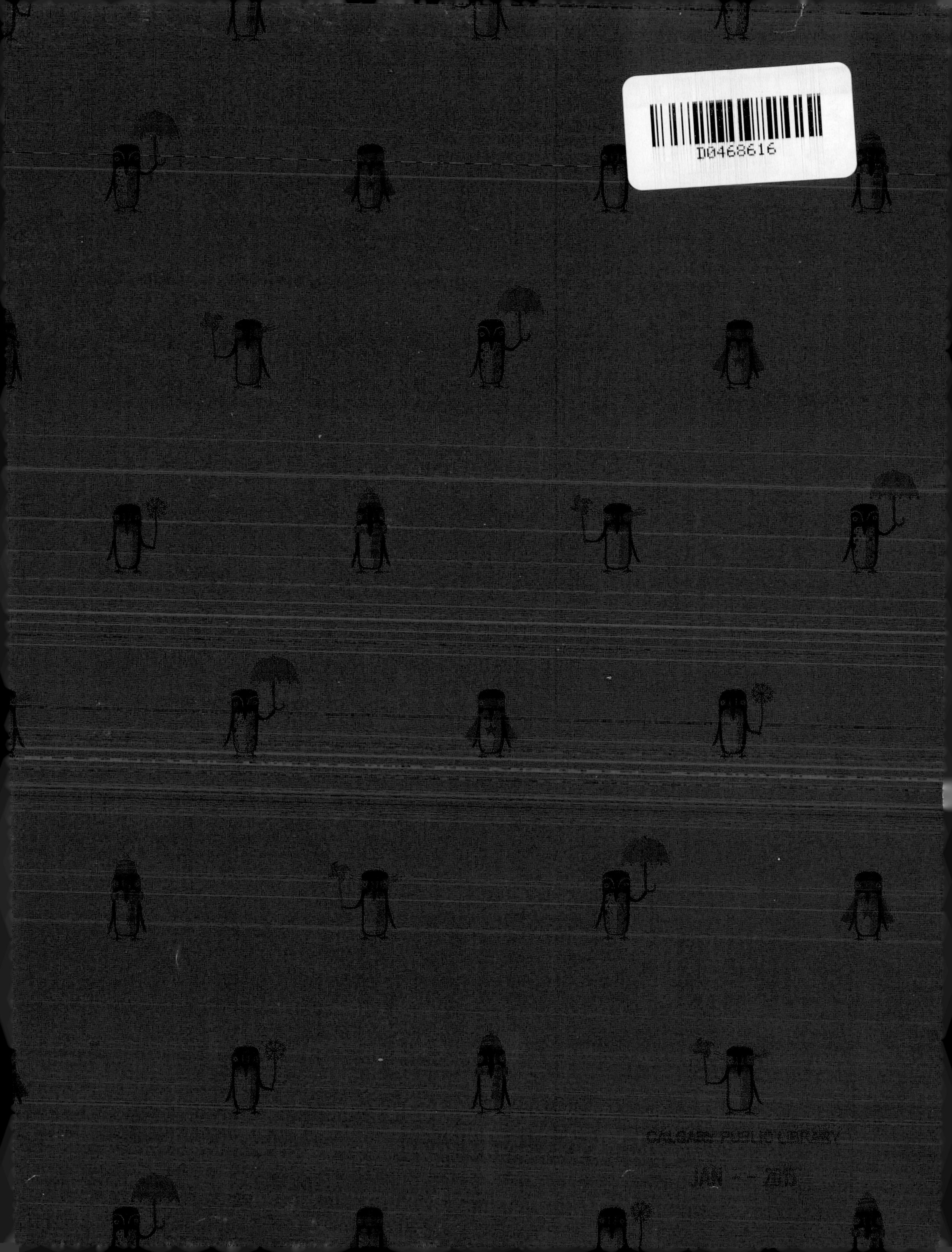

D0468616
CALGARY PUBLIC LIBRARY
JAN

Blown
away

For Ally

Blown Away

For information address HarperCollins Children's Books, a division of HarperCollins Publishers, 195 Broadway, New York, NY 10007.
www.harpercollinschildrens.com

Library of Congress Cataloging-in-Publication Data
Biddulph, Rob, author, illustrator.
Blown away / written and illustrated by Rob Biddulph.
pages cm
Summary: An unexpected adventure with his friends and a kite convinces Penguin Blue that he is not built for flying, and that he belongs on solid ice.
ISBN 978-0-06-236724-2 (hardback)
[1. Voyages and travels—Fiction. 2. Home—Fiction. 3. Flight—Fiction. 4. Zoology—Arctic regions—Fiction. 5. Tropics—Fiction. 6. Arctic regions—Fiction.] I. Title.
PZ8.3.B472Blo 2015
[E]—dc23
2014022227

CIP
AC

The artist used a pencil, some paper, a scanner, Photoshop CS5, a Wacom Tablet, and a Cintiq 6D Art Pen to create the digital illustrations for this book.
14 15 16 17 18 SCP 10 9 8 7 6 5 4 3 2 1
❖
First U.S. edition, 2015
Originally published in Great Britain by HarperCollins Publishers Ltd.

Blown Away

Written and illustrated by

Rob Biddulph

HARPER

An Imprint of HarperCollins*Publishers*

A windy day.
A brand-new kite.
For Penguin Blue
a maiden flight.

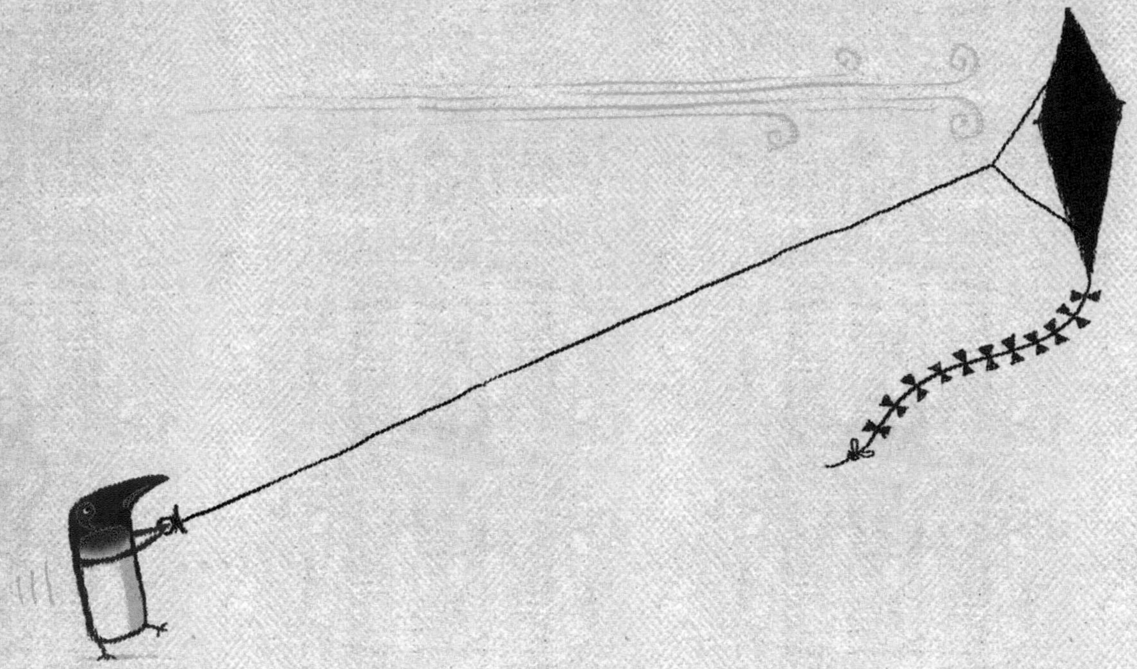

The kite so high. The wind so strong.
It's pulling Penguin Blue along.

"Save me, Penguins Jeff and Flo!"
They try to help, but off they blow.

Up, up, away!
See how they fly—
a penguin-train
up in the sky.

Don't worry,
Wilbur's seen
their plight. . . .

Oh, dear. It seems
he's joined the flight.

Blue spies a bear.
"Oh, help us, do."

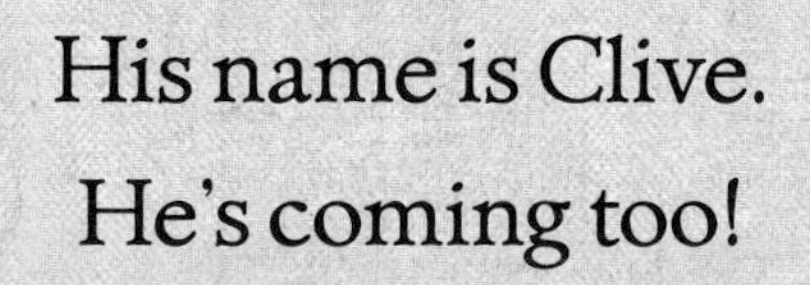

His name is Clive.
He's coming too!

Oh, what a fix!
Oh my! Oh me!
The gang is flying
out to sea!

YOU ARE LEAVING
The ANTARCTIC
PLEASE SWIM CAREFULLY

They swoop, they soar . . . in rain and shine. . . .

They zoom straight through . . . clouds one to nine. . . .

7 8 9

Past miles of
ocean far below.
Then . . . "LAND AHOY!"
shouts Penguin Flo.

A tiny island, lush and green
(a color that they've never seen).
"The trees look soft. We'll be all right.
Hello, jungle! Good-bye, kite!"

"How nice," says Blue.
"A lovely spot,
although it is
a bit too hot."

Jeff misses Mom.

Clive wants to go.

Oh, dear. They can't. They're trapped. Oh, no.

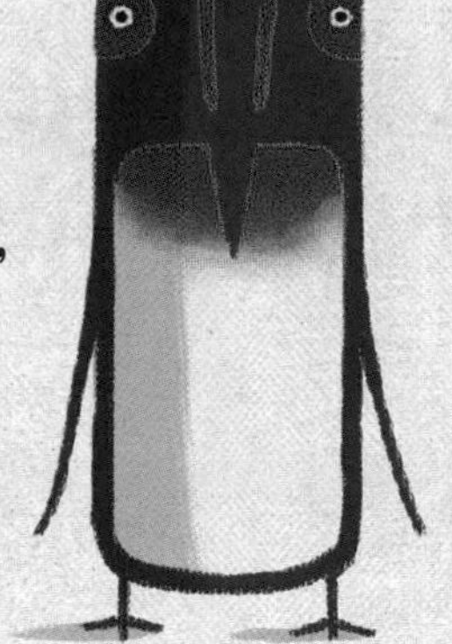

Intrepid travelers, never fear, 'cause Blue has had a good idea.

"The boat,

some leaves,

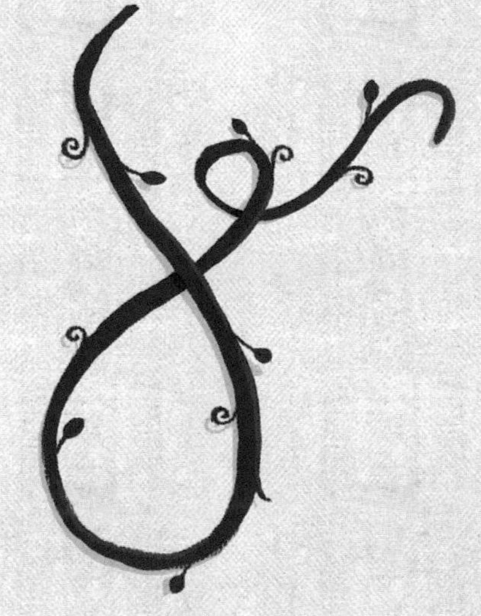

a vine, and then . . .

the wind will blow us home again."

One big gust
should get them going.
Now, who could help?
Who's good at blowing?

WHOO

OSSH!
EVEN MORE SEA

They ride each crest and surf each wave.

Three cheers for five* companions brave.
*Is it five, or is it six? Somebody is playing tricks. . . .

BUS
SCHOOL BUS

At last the chill of home—how nice
to feel your feet on solid ice.

A windy day.
Another kite.
"No thanks," says Blue.
"No trips tonight."

A lesson learned,
there's no denying;
this penguin wasn't
built for flying.

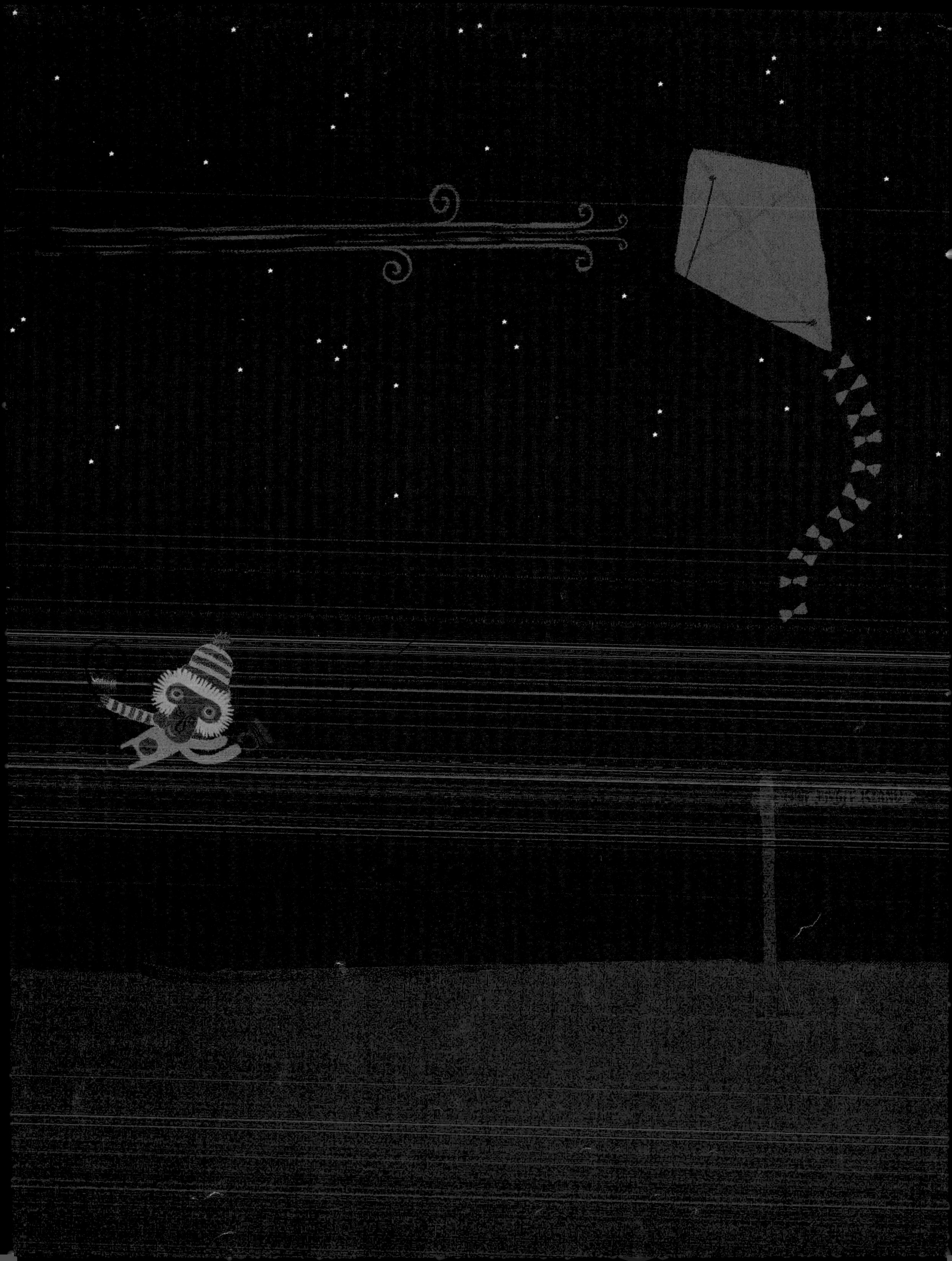